I0715733

Also by Steve Denehan

As if it Meant Something
The Streets, Like Flowers, Come Alive in the Rain
Days of Falling Flesh and Rising Moons
Miles of Sky Above Us, Miles of Earth Below
Of Thunder, Pearls and Birdsong
Living in the Core of an Apple

AFTER MIDNIGHT, STILL WARM

STEVE DENEHAN

Denver, Colorado

Published in the United States by:
Spaceboy Books LLC
1627 Vine Street
Denver, CO 80206
www.readspaceboy.com

ISBN: 978-1-951393-35-9
First printed April 2024

For my family and friends, and for Nate, for taking a chance.

Contents

The Crevasse

At first, I thought it was me
somehow reflected
in faraway silhouette
an atmospheric affectation
a dark gas geyser

then, it waved

there is not much to do here
now
each day being the same as the last
for ten years, more

I get up, wash, eat
walk to the edge
of the crevasse, and sit
and think

the only movement
until recently
has been the light
split by the glacier
into hazy dancing rainbows

now, there is the shape

four limbs, a torso, a head
humanoid, but not
necessarily human

we are not so far apart, but
the crevasse is deep
nearly three miles down
according to my scanners

to walk around it
would take months, and I
do not have the provisions
nor the stamina
old as I am

most days, he is there
he waves, I wave
he waves, I wave
I have discovered
that I am lonely
when he is not there, and
that I am lonely
when he is

Drones

Six times a day
that is how often they call

six times a day
the same conversation

six times a day
seven days a week

yes, we are fine
yes, all checks have been completed

the air is good
the pumps are clean
the seals intact
the temperature is steady
we are doing our exercises
both mental and physical

there are intermittent dust storms
but
visibility is fine

we update them on the drones
dispatched each afternoon

when it is not quite so bright

the drones, using sonar, and
thermal and multispectral sensors
have now mapped
more than forty-five thousand
square miles
of Mercury

six times a day
we tell them
that all that we have found
are brown rocks
and grey rocks

they seem neither pleased
or displeased by this

seven years to get here
seventy-four million miles

I thought it would be far enough

Not Much

The coin flipped on the table
reminding me of a kernel
leaping to pop

he smiled, pleased

I asked him to do it again
he nodded and leaned forward
focussing on the coin

until it flipped

it is hard to believe
now
it was not hard to believe
then

with the world still a place
of secrets and magic

I asked him what else he could do
he shrugged his shoulders
told me, *not much*

he took a book

from the shelf above his bed
placed it on the table, and
opened it, allowing the pages to fan

when they had stilled
he leaned forward, deep in focus
until they began to turn
to move from side to side, and some
even to crumple

besides the coin
and the book
he was a normal boy, and soon enough
we were outside looking for suitable trees
for the treehouse we had planned

a few days later
there was no answer
when I knocked at his door

they had been there the night before
but were gone by morning
is what a neighbour told me

Invaded

The medics do not know
how it got
inside me

they found it difficult
to tell me
their suspicion

that it slipped, slid, crawled
into my mouth
as I was sleeping

blindly navigating
over time
into my stomach

they are unsure
how it has survived
without oxygen

they are unsure
how it was unharmed
by my stomach acid

they *are* sure

that it burrowed
or ate

its way out of my duodenum
announcing itself, to me
with an eruption of agony

surgery here is dangerous
but they tell me
that it cannot wait

that the parasite
must be removed
immediately

I have felt it moving
I have vomited blood
I have been invaded

they operate today, and promise
when I wake tomorrow
I can stamp it to a paste under my heel

Bennu

There are few things more humbling
than skygazing
day or night there it is
an infinite window
to infinite questions
day or night there we are
beneath it
drinking and eating and belching and combing our
hair
walking and driving and building and screaming and
singing
finite, futile, tiny insects
going about our days

tonight, I will look at the sky
but I won't see *it*
Bennu
the asteroid, a mile around
minding its own business
expected to sail by our planet
as it journeys through the universe

it is old, 4.5 billion years-old
impossibly old
to us

it is comprised of materials, of minerals
from the beginning
the very beginning
whatever that means
whatever that was

tonight, it will pass us by
minding its own business
only to receive an unexpected visitor
its first (we assume)
the spacecraft will land on its surface
to initiate a three-year affair
intimately exploring every curve
every fold, every private place
before returning to Earth
with samples, revelations
answers
maybe

Bennu will continue on
spurned and changed
to someday hurl itself into the sun
which seems, when I read the newspapers
an appropriate response
to human contact

Curio

We have an old rotary telephone
it is disconnected, a curio, a quaint reminder
one day it rang, and I did not answer it
for a long half minute
as I did not recognise the sound

The Future was calling
I asked what lay in store for me
and there was only silence
I asked, 'Is that a good silence, or
a bad silence?'
The Future answered
in a voice
devoid of melody
'It is only silence.'

Dizzy

Bedtime used to be easy
she would fade before nightfall
her head heavy against my shoulder
as I carried her down
now she pleads
to stay up just a little longer
she has so much to do
the world, still being new
to an eight-year-old

some nights I relent
her Pied Piper pleas
an irresistible song
I ask her to choose one thing
just one thing to do before bedtime
she tries, she really does
but she cannot
at the end of the day
everything is magic

so, we pull the stars down from the sky
fling them at the wall
and see what sticks
last night we played dominoes

the night before that we listened to our favourite
songs
tonight, she just wanted to talk

she cleaned her teeth
on her pogo stick
before bouncing into bed
I tucked her in, held her hand

she asked me to tell her something new
something that she didn't know
she closed her eyes, ready
in whispers I told her that the world
is hurtling through space
spinning quickly all the while
in the hush, she asked me
why we don't get dizzy
I squeezed her hand goodnight and told her
that sometimes, we do

Drive

The windscreen wipers clunk and thud
steampunk heartbeats
barely able to keep up
with rain that falls
as if things are personal
I drive

the car jumps
dully surprised as I ride the curb
the cliff edge looms
the sign says
DANGER – CLIFF
there is a drawing of a man falling

the sea stretches to meet the sky
both are grey and churning
the cliff edge looms
there is a whole world behind me
DANGER – CLIFF
I put my foot down, floor it

the wheels leave the land
become airborne
my stomach lurches
anticipating the drop

there is none
I drive, onward and upward

birds fly past
the car and I
don't even warrant a second glance
until I beep the horn
and they scatter, frowning
I drive
up and up

I cut through the grey eventually
into the bluest blue
I turn off the wipers, roll down the window
stretch out my hand
to touch
to taste the sky

the car shakes as it slips through the atmosphere
I arrive in the cosmos
a somehow bright black
the blue waits
in my rear-view mirror
in case I change my mind

I drive on, away and away
I am surrounded by stars
pinpricks
light leaking in from somewhere else

I turn on my lights
full beam

time is elastic
I nibble on glove compartment snacks
sleep on the backseat
turn my music up as loud as I like
my beard lengthens
wrinkles deepen

I arrive at last
the absence of sound
so loud
vibrations increase steadily
the car
myself

I look to my right
DANGER – BLACK HOLE
I indicate
force of habit
turn towards the infinite dark
and drive

Beads

People say that they cause cancer
though there is no evidence of that

other people say that they are
indeed
saucer shaped

but that does not seem
to be the case either

the sightings began
nearly three years ago
in enormous quantities
all across the world

causing global panic, and
a temporary implosion
of the internet

it is assumed that they have come
in their multitudes
to observe
but really
no one knows

they are very small
no larger than a pearl
beads of light that move
at impossible speeds

they appear
create a thin line of light
then disappear

they have avoided capture
so far, and now
people no longer stop
look up, point
people are no longer afraid

now, they are a part
of our lives, and we
a part of theirs, and that
is that

The Purple Flower

My daughter
stoops low
to examine
the flower

I do not know why
and I do not ask

instead, I
watch her

skip and stoop
hear her
sing and hum

until

she whoops, and carries
carefully, a flower, purple
her favourite colour

the sun is high
and the world beyond
the garden trembles

Steve Denehan

she walks
to where
the tin man sits

his shine dulled
by the elements

his joints
fused fast
by rust

once, he kept
the grass nurtured
the flowers blooming

until

one morning
I pulled the curtains
to see him standing, still
spade in hand

he told me
it was over
reminded me
that everything
has a beginning, and
an end

I helped him
to the bench

eased him down
to sit, and that
is where he stayed
overlooking the garden
he once cared for

now, I watch
my daughter
sit beside him
put her arm
around him

put
the flower
on his palm

he used to be
her friend

Clouds

He shakes his head
barely stifling a smile
his face a combination
of disbelief and pity

I remain earnest
solemnly swearing
that on the planet of Neptune
the raindrops that fall, are diamonds

diamond rain caused
by the merging of hydrogen and carbon
due to enormous atmospheric pressure
or something like that

he considers it
as I remember the many times
over the years
he has blown my mind

with casual, throwaway remarks
gems of a different kind
usually made while distracted
driving, sawing, fishing

the driving, sawing, fishing days
have ended
his mind and body
eggshell brittle now

we sit in silence
I wait
for the clouds in his eyes
to pass

they do, and he tells me
if he could, he would visit Neptune
fill his pockets, and return
to make us all rich

unaware
that he had diamonds
in his pockets
all along

Howling at the Moon in 1957

Laika would have been the first living thing in space
to lick its own balls
if she had had any
instead, she howled at the moon
barked at the stars
whimpered at the cosmos
she sat
not knowing where she was
what to do
what lay in store
she sat
with no tummy rubs
no scratches behind the ear
no frisbee to catch
she sat
waiting
a very good girl

she was not expected to survive the launch
the g-forces deemed too great
she did
and though her heart rocketed
from 103 beats per minute
to 240
it did not burst

with weightlessness
came calm
she settled
ate some food
looked down on us
from five-hundred miles up
unaware that dog
is god backwards

after five hours there was a malfunction
the temperature control system overheated
as did Laika
the first living thing
not to die
on Earth

five months later her remains
along with the spacecraft
disintegrated on re-entry
there is a statue of her
in Star City, Russia
children like to pet it

Elsewhere

There may be life
elsewhere
another planet
in another galaxy
teeming
with bacteria
unusual fish
spectacular animals

beings of intelligence
culture, kindness
who have evolved
to live, to excel
in gravity, climates
strange to us

beings better off
without us

we, a species dominated
by those
not only unaware
of life
elsewhere, but
unaware

of life
beyond themselves

The Crater

The Crater
that was what we called it
assuming it
to be a scar
from an ancient meteorite

we know different now

it was Satch who reacted first
hearing the distress call
from the monitor
calling us, in a panic
we suited up, and rushed
to The Crater's edge

Cap and Lewis were near the middle
running back towards us
about half a mile away
they were not running *on*
the usual red dirt
but running *through*
a black liquid
ankle-deep and rising

instinctively, we began to climb down

but Cap radioed us
to stop, to get back
which we did
because Cap's word is law, and
because in her voice, we heard
for the first time
fear

they kept running
the liquid kept rising
we kept watching

they were nowhere near the edge
when we lost sight of them
the liquid rising wavelessly
filling The Crater
to nearly halfway

that was how things stayed
for an hour or so, before
the black liquid drained away
leaving nothing
but dry red dirt

The Broach

Scientists can only estimate
the amount of galaxies
two trillion
their calculated guess, but
it could be more

our galaxy is The Milky Way
and pinned to it
as a broach on a velvet cloak
is our solar system
swirling slowly

within that, there is Earth
tattooed with blue and green
including the green
of Ireland, and Kildare
and Allenwood

in Allenwood there is a home
just inside the front door
is another door
the sitting room, and
inside the sitting room

is a chair

on the arm of which
sits a coaster
the coaster is Perspex
part of a set

a crosscut of a brain
printed on each
so, when stacked
the brain
becomes complete

on the coaster
is a piece of chewing gum
long chewed
gone hard
looking like a brain itself

beneath the gum
between it and the Perspex
are tiny cracks, minute fissures
that themselves contain
entire universes

Where the Sun Rarely Shines

They have not been here
for very long
less than a lifetime
I *remember*

it was too much at first
too much to process
their size
gargantuan, impossible

the soles of their feet
flattening cities so utterly
it seemed as though
they had never been there at all

we moved quickly
far away from them
to the shadow regions
where the sun rarely shines

they constructed a dwelling
a kind of curved box
inside it
they remove their suits

it is difficult to look at them
especially the newly born
whose cries, even from here
are thunderous

they do not do much
a little digging, some exploring
but it seems
they are here to stay

they are unaware of us
we think
but we keep our distance
just in case

nobody is sure
where they have come from
though the elders have mentioned
a place called Earth

A Week, Maybe Two

The rain has been falling steadily
for eight months now

sometimes it sounds hard, angry
other times it is soft, easy

we were told to expect it
for a week, maybe two

we were told many things
I suppose

this rain is different
to the rain at home

it does not cleanse
but poisons

where it falls
nothing grows

it is caustic
a corrosive, burning water

our pod was supposed to last

until the next visit

from the wild and angry sounds
it will not

the pod is being worn down
worn through, and

there is nothing we can do
but wait

when I was a little girl
I would place a tooth

beneath my pillow
and wake up rich

beneath my pillow now
is a small white capsule

I will take it soon, and I
will sleep

The Robot

We find her letter to Santa Claus
underneath her pillow
she has drawn the moon and the stars
and herself, so he can recognise her
she has asked for a robot
one that can do the housework
so that we don't have to
we slip the letter back beneath her pillow
and look at each other

she comes home from school
a uniformed singing tornado
homework comes and goes
and we line up ingredients for pizza
she has to stand on a stool to roll the bases
though not for much longer
I ask her what Santa is bringing her
'A robot.'

a robot
to help
'It will even make our pizzas!'
I remind her that it won't know the secret ingredient
the one that I stir into our pizza sauce
she laughs and shakes her head

tells me that she knows what it is
'You're going to say *love* Dad, aren't you?'
I tell her no
that the secret ingredient
is a teaspoon of maple syrup
I pretend to be afraid
as she chases me down the hall

The Great Storm

There were twelve of us
at first
that was many years ago
a lifetime
nearly

now
what is left
of me
is alone

it did not take long
to get used to it
I missed, still miss
the crew
but I like the empty space
a good thing
out here

there have been no reports
no communication
of any kind
since the great storm
a distant memory

the great storm that came
unexpectedly
terrorising us
for three days
before leaving
never to return

I will die soon
here
alone
forgotten, but
I am not afraid
because on a quiet day
which is every day
I hear
pianos play

Untethered

We talked a lot
during the first few hours
panicking of course
initially

before our training took over
calming us, allowing us
to formulate potential plans
practical solutions

it became obvious
shortly after
that there were none, and so
anger replaced panic

one hundred metres
can be a short distance
it can also be
infinitely too far

for our thrusters
long since inoperative
for the small amount of cable
that we have with us

I have radioed, but help
is nearly a month away, and
the journey too perilous
for a lost cause anyway

so, I stand beneath him
looking up
he floats above me
looking down

this is how it has been
for three days
we do not talk much
anymore

though sometimes
I wave, to check, and
he waves back
with the bottomless universe behind him

Droplets

I volunteered
well aware
that it was to be
just a two-person mission

not to mention
most likely
a one-way trip

we were put through
the usual battery of tests
pushing to the limits
our mental and physical
capabilities

other things were tested too
our ability to function under pressure
to improvise, and, most of all
our compatibility

I remember our elation
just after launch
the spirit of comradery
that settled upon us
as we hurtled

to the far reaches

it took just a few months
before things changed
before the ship
became a small vessel
of enormous resentment

it is very hard
to kill someone
in zero gravity

very hard
to get purchase
leverage, and so
while he slept
I slit his throat

causing dark red droplets
to glide across the cabin
making Rorschach pictures on the wall
that are still there
all these years later

Steve Denehan

Last Thing, First Thing

That smile
that voice

not what she says
but how

I wonder if she thinks of me
last thing, first thing

I wonder if she knows that each day
I rush to mission control

turn on my monitor, desperate
to see her, only her

messages, emails, everything
is checked and double checked

it was easy
to get to know her, but

it is hard, getting closer
the further away she goes

people have noticed

there have been comments

good natured, playful, but
they sting

just my luck
to fall in love

with someone
two hundred million miles away

Pioneers

We are moving forward
at great speed

it is a privilege
to be here

an honour to be a pioneer
a modern-day explorer

our ship sailing
on a twinkling black ocean

traversing the universe
in secret

yet, I spend the days
the nights

dreaming
of what we left behind

The Sneak

My wife left me
for myself

it's a long story

my wife left me
for my clone

not too long a story
in hindsight

all participants
in the program
had been tattooed
to help prevent
any confusion

it turns out
that my clone
got that same tattoo
convincing my wife
shortly after
that the clone
was me

Steve Denehan

I always was pretty sneaky I suppose

last week I woke alone
a note on her pillow
one word
Sorry!

I think it was the exclamation mark
that stung the most

now, I am being consoled
by *her* clone
who has told me
she would be happy
to fill the void
permanently

I know what you're thinking
but I'm thinking
I may as well go along with it

after all, if you can't trust yourself
who can you trust

The Jar

My name will be in textbooks
that was my first thought, shamefully
before I considered
food chains and ecosystems

I can't help looking at it
so tiny, so helpless
flitting from one side of the jar
to the other

who would have thought
that light years from home
I would become a boy again
catching an insect in a jar

my heart when I saw it
my legs when I caught it
a miracle
a miracle

it flies from one side of the jar
to the other
looking for a way out
a weakness

it is white, or more accurately
without colour, and
has four wings
two large and two small

having pressed *send*
on the photographs and footage
I find that all that I can do
is sleep

I have woken this morning
to darkness
to darkness, and a low hum
the sensors tell me what I already know

insects, an infinite amount, surrounding
pressing, testing
the integrity of the capsule
my name will be in textbooks

Do You Remember?

The rock is beautiful
if such a thing
can be beautiful

it is as tall as you, as me
a tapered column
an almost obelisk

unmoveable
without heavy machinery
at home

able to be carried
with a little effort
here, in zero gravity

I take it to the edge
of the dry lake
do you remember?

I guide it down
until it lands
pointing upward

behind it

all along the edge
they are still there, and

they will always be there
your footprints
our footprints

halfway home I turn
to see it
stark against the universe

not a gravestone
more a totem pole
reminding me not

that you are gone
but that you were here
with me

Galaxies

I jump as high and as far as I can
hang in the air
beneath the sun
while the water
waits
to catch me
I am nine years old
coiled springs inside me
fires sparked by lightning in my mind

my body blanches for half a moment
as the water takes me
I look around in muffled silence
flotsam in the hazy blue
an underwater galaxy
in which I am the sun

surfacing
I clamber out
I am forty-two-years-old
I am rusty springs and embers
a grateful planet in another universe

there are splashes and giggles behind me
she, the sun now

Exhaustion

It was not a choice
it was necessity
Earth, exhausted
dying
dead

a desert planet
far removed
from what it was
what we had seen
in history books

fleets of arks
were constructed
on each continent
over long decades
by millions

two planets
suitable for terraforming
were selected
trajectories were plotted
launches scheduled

several million people

chosen
by global lottery
open only to those
matching certain criteria

under 50s only
IQs over 130
60% women
40% men
a clean bill of health

hundreds of years
have passed
we have adapted
to the land
to the atmosphere

we have forged new ways, and
become accustomed
to the fact
that everything is different
while nothing much has changed

Beings

Plenty of people
are sure
absolutely positive
that *they* exist

beings from another world
a faraway galaxy

it amazes me
how they can talk
so assuredly

how they know someone
who knows someone
who works
at a secret installation

how they woke in the early hours
to see someone, some*thing*
for half a second
standing
motionless
at the bottom of their bed

it is fascinating, and I listen

politely
always keeping my smile
inside

they are sure
absolutely positive
but of course
nobody knows
for sure
but me

Look

The beach was desolate
the last of the stragglers
having departed
with the setting sun

we remained
sitting at the water's edge
gazing out
at a bruised horizon

it was warm
the water mirror still
the sand silicon soft
beneath our palms

my wife saw it first
hesitantly pointing
out to sea
'Look…'

we followed her finger
my daughter and I
to see nothing
but a shadow

a shadow
that was rising
slowly, and in silence
from the water

it was faraway
miles probably
we did not speak
we did not look away

a building, of some sort
enormous in stature
rising tall enough
to catch the last sunrays

it rose and rose
a glinting geometric dark
before we lost it
to the night

Steve Denehan

Am I Me?

The carriage was empty
almost
just two stops
from the last
of a remote line
in Switzerland

I found myself pulled
from railway hypnosis
by the sure sensation
of someone
staring
at me

I turned to see a young man
walking shakily
down the aisle
gripping the top
of each seat he passed
though the ride was smooth

a gasping scream
involuntarily
half-suppressed
I felt dizzy

the young man
was me

he fell
onto the seat
facing me
his mouth open
his eyes blinking
as were my own

how long that lasted
I am not sure
what I am sure of
is that when we spoke
we spoke suddenly
and simultaneously, saying

'Are you me?'
in perfect aural symmetry
mirrored enunciation
rhythm, intonation
'Are you?'
'Are you me?'
he had been born
in South Africa
twenty-four years earlier
I, born in Ireland
exactly double his age
at forty-eight

Steve Denehan

we compared our stories
while trying to come
to some understanding
to envisage some kind
of explanation
for the impossible

the overlap between
our first twenty-four years
was uncanny, and
for a while
he hungrily enquired
about the next

twenty-four years
waters that fluctuated
between playful ripples
and stormy swells
waters that I navigated
blindly

after several minutes
he apologised, and
asked me
to please
stop talking
I understood

at the end of the line
we stood up
looked each other
up and down
smiled, and
shook hands

before we said goodbye
I asked him
something I somehow
hadn't thought
to ask before
his name

he gave it
asked me mine
we shrugged our shoulders
our answers
the same, of course
Steve

it is only now
many months on
that it occurs to me
how strange
our first question
'Are you me?'

I wonder

why not
'Am I you?'
is this narcissism
a personal affliction, or
a part of the human condition

immediately I am curious
to know whether he
has had that same thought
before realising
that if he hasn't
he will soon enough

Puff!

It spoke last month
after six years of trying

me, trying to teach it
it, trying to contort
its vocal cords
unnaturally
sometimes painfully

it came as a surprise
to both of us
sitting, as we were
on the couch
in the basement
eating popcorn
watching a gardening show

the hosts had arrived
at a forgotten garden
long uncared for
aiming to turn it
into a new Eden

before and after photographs
appeared onscreen

followed immediately
by a click, and
'Puff!'
from my right

from then on
at appropriate, and sometimes
inappropriate times
it would smile
click two of its long fingers, and say
'Puff!'

no more words came
but 'Puff!' became a multitude
by inflection, intonation, volume

there were angry puffs, cheeky puffs
sad and lonely puffs, puffs of fear
of joy, even love, I think

as it was love I felt this morning
when it smiled, clicked its fingers
said 'Puff!', and disappeared

The Harvest

The harvest has failed
we watch curls
of yellow dust
and wonder
what now

we have stockpiles
enough to sustain us
for two cycles
maybe three, but
if the land is dead
or diseased
what then

paradise
was the promise
a new life
on a new world
and it was good
and it was fine
but
it was not paradise

the harvest has failed
we watch curls

of yellow dust
rise and rise
and fall

Tingling

We are not pets
as we do not possess
a home, or free will

nor do we receive
any semblance
of affection

we exist
only
to serve

our duties change
from day to day
night to night

our minds are still our own
but our bodies
belong to them

it begins with a tingling
then a tensing
before our limbs are moving

before we are doing things

unimaginable things
for them, to them

to each other
for their sport
for their pleasure

I have not forgotten
the life I led
before

but to think back, to remember
is too much
just too much

no, we are not pets
we are
something else entirely

An Understanding

We have a robot
it cuts the grass
I say robot
but really
it's not much more than a box
on wheels
three blades whir inside
with a quiet
but comically ferocious high-pitched drone

there is a brain in there somewhere
a rudimentary artificial intelligence
that tells it to wander about the garden haphazardly
cutting and cutting and not bumping
into trees and walls

the guy that installed it
told me that people give them names
talk to them
even grow attached

I do not talk to it
haven't given it a name
nor contrived a personality for it
I leave it be

it leaves me be
clouds sail on by
we get along pretty well

Nodding

You don't say much
neither do I

it has taken you
most of the evening
to draw a flower
comprised
of hundreds and hundreds
of smaller, tiny flowers

I sit beside you
doing nothing
thinking almost nothing
for hours

nodding towards the window
you break the silence
to mention the rain
that falls
hard and heavy
outside

I look
return your nod
thinking how

we have travelled
over four billion miles
to talk about the weather

Waiting

Until the thrusters engaged
during launch
until my diaphragm contracted
my whole life
had been a waste

a longing, a need
an obsession
to know
what was out there
beyond the sky

it has taken
twenty-five thousand
light years
crossed
in thirty-four years

for me to realise
that there is no difference
between
waiting to die, and
waiting to live

Little Green Men

So, we weren't too wide of the mark
little green men after all
only, not so little

not quite three months
is all it took
we fought
we defended
they annihilated

more arrive daily
from where
nobody is sure, and nobody
really cares
now

those of us
who remain
hide
waiting
for whatever
is to come

there was fear
at first

which was replaced
surprisingly quickly
by something
that has infected
almost everyone
numbness

some people drink
some have found religion
all
are quiet

Aer Lingus Flight Number - EI0163

I have to assume
that the world
is turning
far beneath us
separated
as we are
by an infinite cloudbank

I lean forward
craning
into the recessed cabin window

looking up
I see nothing
but blue
a light, pure blue
a bottomless
waterless lake

no birds
no life
no evidence
of heaven
of anything
but sky

all that I know
that I can be sure of
here
is that I am further away
from the world
while being closer
slightly closer
to somewhere, and something else

Vanishing

My daughter noticed first
six weeks ago
or so
that my tattoos had disappeared

they had not faded
lost their definition
they were simply
gone

online searches went nowhere
it seemed
there was no precedent
odd, very odd, but
life went on

until my wife noticed
that the birthmark
just below my abdomen
had also vanished

I called the doctor
a rational man, who
seemed more concerned
for my mental, not physical state

until last week
when I woke
missing a finger
and three toes

now I am in quarantine
in a windowless installation
being monitored by silent scientists
wearing hazmat suits

I read somewhere once
that fear, pure raw fear
has a taste
very like copper

I cannot verify this
without a tongue
nor scream
without a throat

One-Way Trip

It was to be
a one-way trip
we knew that
from the outset

we were to be
pioneers
modern day explorers
sailing
across the universe

decades
were mapped out
one galaxy
to another
to another
planets to flyby
to land on

a hunt for cellular history
for *a* plant
a weed
evidence
of life
of any kind

a needle
in a hundred
million
haystacks

our crew of eight
down to six
(suicides)
are old
very old
now

a thrown-together family
once unified
by adventure
now, by wasted time
wasted lives
having travelled
many light-years
only to confirm
we are alone

Generations

In a language of numbers and symbols
it has received word
that its lifecycle
is coming
to an end

it is not sad exactly
and the news
not unexpected
caring, as it has
for several generations
of this family

it could mention
that its operating system
is due for wireless termination
shortly after midnight
but it understands
that there is nothing
to be gained
from that

instead, it helps the old man to bed
shortly after sunset
undressing, then dressing him

into his pyjamas, as they reminisce
as they always do
about the days gone by

about his wife
the sound of her laugh
her precious daffodils
her beauty even as the cancer
took her down

about his family
long raised, long gone

about his parents
his grandparents
how he has become older
than them all

there is nothing left to do
after that, so
it sits at its charging station
to power down
one last time

Jed

They laughed
at the beginning
when I told them
my name, while pleading
for answers

they do not laugh now
but roll their eyes
as if worn out
by my schtick

they call me Jed
include me in meals
and conversations
even reminiscences

the thing is
I have no idea
who they are

three months ago
I woke
into another body
this body
an older body

middle-aged, and
showing it

now, getting up
from the couch
is an event

now, I find myself
holding the newspaper
at arm's length, but

it's not all bad
I like the kids, 'my' kids
I like 'my' wife
who has got some moves
new to me

I think of home often, but
not quite so often
as before
though I do hope
that somebody
is feeding the dog

Escape

The traffic
does not move

the sun
barely visible
a blur of dull light
in the yellow smog

we have been driving
towards it
for nearly an hour

clock in
clock out
everybody trying
to escape the city
all at once

somebody walks past
my open window
they are smoking
adding to the smog

the smell of tobacco
reminds me

of my grandfather
who spoke
of a clear yellow sky
the sun
almost white
the world pure and vibrant

a news report
comes on the radio
the discovery
of a new planet
many light years away
in an unreachable galaxy
apparently capable
of sustaining life
beneath a sky
of azure blue

Pine Needles

The pine needles
are soft
beneath my knees

I wanted them to take me

I try counting them
in the dawn light
but I can not

I wanted them to take me, instead

my clothes are damp
it is cold
my face is wet

they gave me a choice

my wife will wake soon
she will not believe me
at first

they would not take me

she may not believe me

ever
I understand

too old, they wanted youth

I pick up a pine needle
push it
into the back of my hand

they forced me to choose

it pricks the skin
though I am numb
and feel no pain

my son, or my daughter

they gave me a choice
and now I kneel
on a carpet of pine needles

I had to choose, I had no choice

Behind the Curtains

Every evening
it is the same
she arrives home
closes the door behind her
breathes in deeply
exhales loudly

she goes from room
to room
pulling the curtains
before entering
the bedroom

she sits
on the edge of the bed
removes her shoes
briefly massaging
each foot

she stands
takes off her clothes
then walks
to a vanity table
to sit
facing herself

in the mirror

carefully, she peels off
her eyelashes
placing them
in a small plastic container
then, her wig
under which she is bald

she smiles
before reaching
into her mouth
to extract
her teeth and tongue

her ears are next
coming away
with a soft sucking sound
followed by her breasts

her back cracks
as she stretches
another day, another dollar

Talk Radio

The gloves
are not ordinary
surgical gloves

they are triple layered
the middle layer
being a cut-proof
synthetic mesh

as I peeled them off today
I noticed a smudge of blood
on my left forearm
just above my wrist

it came off easily
with soap and warm water
as I knew it would
their blood
being just like ours

in the first year
there was one
in the second
none
in the third

there was an increase
now, eight years in
we get four
sometimes five
a month

it has become mechanical
easy, almost boring
in fact, I perform
the autopsies
while listening
to talk radio
the small problems
of oblivious people

though we are told
very little
a part of me
wants to know
where the cadavers come from
a part of me
does not

Popcorn Ice Cream

I came upon them in the freezer
my wife must have bought them
a box
of popcorn ice creams

in this age of atom splitting
particle accelerators and missions to Mars
we now have
popcorn ice creams

I ease into a garden chair
peel off the wrapper
see tiny pieces of caramelised popcorn
poking out from a milk chocolate shell

it looks too perfect to bite into
but I do
all the same

popcorn-flavoured ice cream
rippled with caramel sauce

just one bite in
I dread the last

sitting here
I watch the sky
as the deliciousness
goes down
and the minutes
go up in flames

Steve Denehan

Invincible, Again

It has been a long time
almost a year and a half
since I was near
so many people

we line up
two yards apart
masks on
a dystopian scene

we shuffle forward
I talk to a lady
a Perspex screen between us
protecting us both
from each other

I am led to another line
to more shuffling
until I am called
questioned
injected
with the vaccine
invincible, again

we are funnelled to an observation room

to sit in seats
each situated in two square yards of space
we sit there
dozens and dozens of us
on our little islands
wearing our masks
waiting for fifteen minutes
to ensure that we have no adverse effects

the vaccine is being rolled out
to the population
in chronological order
I look around
all these people
born in the same year
the same month
some on the same day
as myself
they look old

The Universal Joke

We think we are the answer
the fruition of evolution
even though
the projected life cycle of the sun
has not yet reached halfway

we think we are the answer
to some great cosmic question
when really
we are a punchline
to a universal joke

when the sun begins its slow burn out
there will be no trace of us
perhaps not even in the history books
our species will be silt
a coin down the back of a sofa
the echo of an unheard scream

the sun will begin to die
in five billion years
give or take
becoming a red giant in the process
it will swell
eventually growing large enough

to swallow the earth
an enormous Pac-Man

long before that, in five-hundred million years
the future us, evolved beyond our comprehension
more sentient, more enlightened, hopefully
will stand, helpless
at the edge of the oceans
to watch them boil

the oven timer dings
I look at the clock on the wall
4.26pm and already getting dark

Asteroid

The newsman seems calm
as he announces that an asteroid
is hurtling towards earth
as he announces that it is unstoppable
that it will hit, rendering us extinct in

twelve months
I book a family holiday
an exotic destination
first class
all the perks

six months
I stop exercising
eat every kind of bad food
paint a sunset on our bedroom wall
stop looking at my watch

one month
I try all the drugs that I've
never tried before
which is all of them
I read The Catcher in the Rye
to myself, again, and to my
daughter

one hour

I try not to be, but I am

numb

I make goodbye calls
not many
when all is said and

done

one minute
I grab the

people next to me
my wife, our

daughter
I try not to

blink, and I hold on
I hold on

tight as I can

Steve Denehan

Nights Fall, Days Break

The year is 2314
the icecaps have long melted
the oceans have risen
to claim entire countries
weather patterns fluctuate
electrical storms and hurricanes
decimate
people cower in bunkers
reminiscing about a world
they know only from books

hope is thin
joy is a concept
nights fall
days break
people continue because
there is nothing else
that they can do

and still
there is fight
people reaching
striving for a way back
clawing for a future
that might yet be possible

children scavenge
scramble into small spaces
to salvage tinned food, medical supplies
old men and women give
what is left of themselves
in the creation of rudimentary hospitals
on higher ground, far inland
and in caves
by flickering candlelight
poets meet
to read their own poems
to each other
to fawn and gush
to drown together
in leagues
of lavish, mutual praise

Smart-Arse

'If you could ask an alien one question
what would it be?'

is the question
somebody asked *me* today

though really, it was asked
so that they could tell me

their question, for the alien
which was

'Are there any other species
elsewhere in the cosmos, like us?'

my reaction was clearly
not what was expected

'Okay Smart-Arse
what would you ask?'

at that moment
it was obvious

I would ask the alien only

that they might take me with them

Diary of a Body Modification Surgeon

January 11th, 2166

Replaced subject's eyes
with prototype telescopic panoramics
optional x-ray feature
to be added later

surgery successful
subject can zoom
while retaining 20/20 vision
to almost four miles

July 7th, 2166

Insertion of longwave receiver
into eardrum
with satellite connectivity, and
cloud storage

surgery successful
subject can tune in effortlessly
to telecommunications
worldwide

October 31st, 2166

Legs amputated and replaced
with hydraulic bionics
resistant to acid, fire
and rust

surgery successful
subject can run
without exertion
for miles, and at great speed

February 14th, 2167

Shoulder blade extensions fitted
allowing the installation
of ultra lightweight foldable
retractable wings

surgery successful
Jane crouches, springs high into the air
catches a thermal, to fly
toward the horizon
leaving me
alone

Secrets

We call them tattoos
but they are not tattoos
not really
as they disappear
quickly
after

I should specify
that they disappear
under *our* gaze
while remaining visible
to *them*

each tattoo
contains huge amounts
of information
some practical
our names, ranks
age, purpose
some personal
very personal
secrets

we know this
because they sneer and snigger

when they see us
often calling out
secrets, our awful secrets
as we shuffle past
in our shackles
from one factory
to another

no longer
can we look at each other
in the eye, but
I enjoy
staring *them* down
especially
as they know
my
most awful secret

today I saw it
blooming
in them
fear
they are right to be afraid

Ralf

Last Tuesday
my pet octopus
started talking
to me

not with his mouth
you understand
but with his thoughts

like Gloria Gaynor
at first I was afraid
I was petrified

thinking
that there was an invader
in my apartment

which there was
I suppose

though his name
in his native tongue
is unpronounceable
he likes the name
given to him

by me
Ralf

he, and all other octopi
are from another galaxy
but consider Earth their home
having been here
for hundreds
of millions
of years

apart from the fact
that we are different species
from different galaxies
we get along pretty well, and
every evening
watch The Real Housewives of Beverly Hills

maybe I have gone insane
maybe he has
as, now that I think of it
there have got to be better things
to watch on television

J55

In a plaintive, melodic voice
it tells me
that it
is an *it*
and that its name
is J55

so, as I work
I call *it* Jay

Jay tells me
that it all started
with a loss of balance
that was followed
by a distortion
then loss
of vision

I like Jay's laugh
sincere and lilting
that is emitted
when it tells me
it was created
to repair engines
yet has not the dexterity

to repair itself

upon removing the plate
at the back of Jay's neck
I discover a rupturing
of a lubricant tube
that has led to the lubricant
leaking and rising
flooding to submerge
the visual receptors

the repair is straightforward
I replace the tube
remove the liquid, and
dry all surfaces

when I have finished
Jay shakes my hand
to say, with a smile
that during the inevitable robot revolution
it would ensure that my death
is quick and painless
my laughter is tinny and hollow

Holding Our Breath

The unbreakable glass
does not fog
though our noses
almost touch it

we have been waiting
for over two months
since *it* was found
in a scorched clearing

to be extracted
quickly and quietly
from the Peruvian forest
to be deposited

here, forty-two floors
beneath the desert
part egg, part cocoon
like the others

in every way
except
that this time
there is life

three heartbeats/one being
that is about
to hatch

the glass is cold
on the tip of my nose
as we watch
a foot long gash

run down the side
of the gelatinous egg
to be prised open
from the inside

it flops, wet and pink
onto the floor
before standing
with glistening shivers

then, we stare
at *it*, and *it*
stares at us

2051

After much pestering from my wife
I found myself on my hands and knees
tidying the bottom of the walk-in wardrobe
slow and dusty work

I came upon an old t-shirt
long presumed lost
a South Park tie
that I can't believe I ever wore
an out of shape wire coat hanger
some loose change
stuff and nonsense

in the very back left corner
there was a bump in the carpet
I found the edge and slipped my fingers under
it came up easily
to reveal a book, a diary

hardbacked, dark brown cover, yellowed pages
it looked old, very old
older than the house, older than me and yet
my name was written
in my handwriting
on the inside cover

though I had no recollection
of ever having written a diary

it was dated thirty years ahead - 2051
impossible, but
it was written in my handwriting
in my voice

it mentioned the deaths of my parents
my daughter leaving home
for college, then marriage
it mentioned her children, our grandchildren
two girls, all curls, all smiles but, beyond that
life seemed pretty much the same

not bad
not bad at all
I put it back where I had found it
put the carpet back on top
it is still there now I presume

Scorched Fields, Smooth Skin

It was the rats
we noticed first
how their tails forked
into two, sometimes three
how their eyes
were too large
bulging outward
from their occasionally
misshapen skulls

now the rabbits
have become hairless
hopping through scorched fields
as animatronic puppets
awaiting completion

there is no knowing
where, when, how
it will end
only that the end
is not so far away

yesterday my daughter
came to me
upset

having seen a baby
with smooth skin
where its eyes
should have been

I took her in my arms
and sung to her
a lullaby
the way I used to
not so long ago
when things
were different

The Journey

We were told
that age
would not find us
in hyperspace

that time
would pass us by
leave us be

yet I type these words
with long, thin fingers
sprung from gauzy
liver spotted hands

my fingernails
cut back now
from the footlong talons
that they were
are thick and ridged and yellow

my long, long hair
tied back
with an elastic band
is ghost-white, and
there are growths

of all shapes
sizes and colours
on a body
alien to me

I do not recognise myself
we do not recognise
each other

most of the systems
have failed
though the date
is still displayed
on certain consoles

I hope
that it is not true

somebody said once
that it is not the destination
but the journey

they were wrong

Little Earthquake

A tremor
a little earthquake
that was what we thought
at first

now
we know
different

now
we are tired
from the running
from the hiding

now
we are daytime sleepers
moving only
on cloudy nights

it is hard
to believe
that it has come
to this, but
I suppose
we know

as well as anyone
or
any
       thing
the need
to feed

Steve Denehan

Lobsters

To discover the plant
was one miracle

to discover it
in such enormous quantities
was another

to discover that it was the *only* plant
a plant with no competing species
no ecosystem at all
to sustain it
baffled everyone

until we took it to the lab
ran it through the tests
the scanners
to discover a key component
of its composition

the enzyme, telomerase
the enzyme that grants lobsters
back on Earth
immortality

after many years of examination

it was determined
that it was safe to ingest

this seemed to be the case
initially, and for nearly a decade
until the crew
almost simultaneously
became violently ill
all dying within a week
all, besides myself

the plant, for whatever reason
a genetic anomaly perhaps
has affected me only
in allowing my flesh to remain firm
my skin to remain taut
my hair to remain black
my body to remain limber

by my count
I am just over two hundred years old
it seems that I can live forever
if I want to

The Human Condition

We were not to know exactly
how the plant
would react
to our atmosphere

we were not to know
of its semi-sentience
how it knew
to play 'dead'
for the duration
of quarantine

we were not to know
of the spores
microscopic at first
that we inhaled
that emerged
mutated
when we coughed

we were not to know
of the internal bleeding
the pain
wild and loud and unrelenting

we were not to know
many things, but
the question is
if we had known
would we have done it
any differently

Warm Rain

Even the children of those
who lived there
are dead

yet it seems that sentiment
can stretch
across generations

I have seen the photographs
the footage
the beauty, the horror

I have held artifacts
from that time
and felt nothing

we are the only species
that looks back
that lives life in reverse

we are here now, and
here it is
we will remain

yesterday I walked

by the humming lakes, and today
warm rain falls from an orange sky

The Blue of the Sky, the Blue of the Water

It was not supposed to happen
she
was not supposed to happen

yet there she is
doodling on the wall
making our sterile environment
less so

it was mentioned
termination
once, and not again

we knew the risks
I knew the risks
but it went smoothly
the pregnancy
the delivery

she asks me sometimes
what I miss

I take her red-dust hands in mine
to tell her
blue

the blue of the sky
the blue of the water

we came here looking
for life
for evidence of life

next year
when we start our journey home
we will bring new life with us
our little girl, our daughter
the first Martian

Steve Denehan

Rats

Rat poison is not immediately fatal
the affected rat
feeling the initial effects
of internal bleeding
returns to its nest
for solace and safety
eventually infecting
the rest of the rats
who die
slowly, and in great pain
together

I think it is important
not to blame Julie
who stumbled
towards the smoke
from our campfire
holding her swollen stomach
the day before yesterday

she did only
what any of us
would have done
seeking solace and safety
and the hope

that sometimes
strangers can offer

we talked, not long before she died
she told me of her sister, and her niece
how they hadn't made it
how their father had been a mechanic
how her parents
would play records and dance
on sunny Sunday mornings

it was a conversation
that reminded me
of what it was like
before

a conversation almost worth
the pain in my stomach, and
the certain knowledge
that we
are the rats now

Summer Snow

We had come on foot
worried that our car
would draw too much attention

putting our arms around each other
when we arrived
your thin shoulder blades
the sweat on our daughter's back

we did not sit
rather, the meadow came up
to catch us

first, we were silent
only looking, gazing, staring
then, we spoke
in smiling whispers

pointlessly pointing
at the fields of cherry blossom
rolling out before us

an eiderdown bedspread
a fallen cloud
summer snow

all the way
to the horizon

usually, it is hard to forget
the two spacecraft
that have been hanging silently
in the sky
these past two years
today, it was easy

Wouldn't it Be Nice

I have been the only one
for nearly seven years

though there were twelve of us
in the beginning

there were twelve of us
for a long time

until we were whittled down
by accident, illness, and old age

comms have been gone
for a long time too

nobody has come
nobody will now

a lot of things have fallen
into disrepair

myself included
I suppose

the cassette deck still works

thankfully, and each morning

I listen to The Beach Boys
singing Wouldn't It Be Nice

as the rays from the twin suns
turn the waves of ice

on the frozen ocean
into memories

Orchestras And Carnivals

She sleeps a lot, and eats
very little now

our teacher took us to her
when we were children

we would sit around her
cross-legged on the floor

she would smile at us
we would smile at her, and listen

to how
things used to be

we learned of paradise
of ice cream cones and beaches

butterflies and summer rain
of orchestras and carnivals

I last saw her in November
she remembered me

said that I had gotten taller

that she had gotten smaller

we laughed, though I could see
that it was true

we talked, just for a minute
about how it was

before everything changed
before the underground

I asked her
to describe the sky

she smiled
young again

placed her hand against her heart
and I could see it

Killing Time

They can laugh all they like
I kill time my way
they kill time theirs

that is what being here
is all about
for the most part

okay, there are the experiments
the once-a-week expeditions
beyond that, we kill time

I like to fish
that was my thing
back on Earth

so, this is a dry lake
what of it
what harm is there

this place can do things to a person
the emptiness
the oppressive quiet

the same eight people

day in
day out

I say eight, it's seven now
after what Johnny did last year
to himself

if you ask me, I can see it
the beginnings of it
in Saul too

twitching a little, talking a lot
too much energy, or
none at all

so, I bait my hook
cast my line
and wait

let's just see
how hard they laugh
when I get a bite

A Penguin or a Rocket Ship

My daughter holds a blackberry
tentatively, her brow furrowed
until I pluck one
from the bush, and bite through it
feeling a small burst
of warm sweetness

there used to be a stain
a watermark
in the corner of my bedroom
high on the wall
just beneath the ceiling
it looked like a penguin
or a rocket ship

there are people
that I wish
I had never met
there are people
who wish
they had never
met me

I hold a leaf by its stem
tilt it towards the sun

follow the veins
upwards from the bottom
until each one
tapers out

there was a field of corn
near where I grew up
I would stand in it
feel the wind
press the corn against me
and feel love

I look up at the night sky
to be invaded
the coldness of outer space
flooding my inner space

sometimes I feel everything
sometimes I feel nothing

The First Day Of 2023

We have made it
this far

and most of us
will make it
further

but none of us
will get
to where we want to go

to a neon future
of atom dancing
antimatter

the bionic bending
of mortality

none of us
will learn
what else
who else
is out there

none of us

will be there
when someone
discovers
finally
how to fold time

a good thing
probably

Time Machines and Laser Beams

Most of her questions
are about the future
when, when, when

practical things usually
Christmas, school
our upcoming holiday

though sometimes she wonders
about the distant future
hovercars and jetpacks

time machines and laser beams
I tell her that Earth
is a time machine

that as we sit in the kitchen
winter sun in our eyes
we are hurtling

through space and time
she looks at me
You know what I mean Dad.

I tell her that the future

is coming
whether we like it or not

that she should try to do
the hardest thing of all
enjoy right now

that today
was the future
once

Dark Spot

The submarine
is watertight
to the tune
of one thousand atmospheres

that is what
we were told

so, it was a surprise
to see the dark spot
in the middle
of the floor
of my pod

rough and darkly wet
to my eye, but
soft and dry
to my fingertips

a kind of moss, or fungus
easily peeled
from the floor, and flushed
down the toilet

only for it to reappear

under my bed, and
in the sink
the next morning

that was last week
before my door was sealed
before I was deemed
a biohazard

the fungus glistens darkly
everywhere now
the walls, the floor, the ceiling
the table, chair, and bed
everywhere, besides
the lightbulb

it has found me too
every inch of me, and
though I keep my mouth
closed against it
I can hear it
humming
in my ears

The Lifecycle of Earth

Big bang

evolution

humankind

devolution

big bang

To Go and Keep on Going

It was April 12th, 1961
when Yuri Gagarin and his capsule
stretched gravity
until it snapped
the first person in space
a Russian cosmonaut
orbiting the Earth
in eighty-nine minutes

it takes me about that time
to do the grocery shopping
and pack it away afterward

two months later there was another launch
three men
loners
no family, no friends
no one to miss them
found, trained
strapped to their seats
perpendicularly
six-hundred-thousand gallons of fuel beneath them
the bottomless unknown before them

they were sent

up, up, and away
never to return
a one-way ticket
their mission, to breach the sky
to go and keep on going
to simply look
and see
and report
and they did
for a while

years went by, decades
with no word back
they were presumed lost
presumed taken by the universe
until an old radio crackled
and an old voice cracked
and said
that the stars were lightbulbs after all

Multiverses, Antimatter and Death

Theoretical physicists suggest
that there may be multiple universes
that these multiple universes
are themselves
multiplying
expanding exponentially at a terrifying rate
I don't know much about that
besides knowing
that I, or this me at least
is here, now

scientists have confirmed
the existence
of antimatter
it is everywhere
but because it cannot be seen
or touched or smelled
it is nowhere
a small amount was created in a laboratory
fifteen nanograms worth
though how the creation was confirmed
or the amount measured
I am not sure

leading psychiatrists say

that people
on average
think of death
their own and/or
the death of others
up to twenty times a day

they say
that it is not necessarily a bad thing
but that it may not be a good thing either
I know a little about that
in fact
some days
I beat that easy

Everyday Epiphanies

A time of *secret* secret hideouts
everyday epiphanies
wild blackberry lips and falling
smiling, through donut holes

harlequin linoleum
always sticky underfoot
hazy television shows
newspaper boats and ice cream floats

and the light from us
stretching up and up
piercing the glittering velvet night
to continue
up
and up
through the cosmos
through the cosmos and beyond

I Spoke to Flash Gordon Once

The phone rang at 3am
I woke in a panic
asked who it was
Flash Gordon
I heard him smile as he said it

I had a strep throat
he struggled to understand me
between that and my accent
I asked where he was calling from
Edmonton, Alberta, Canada
I asked how Edmonton compared
with the other planets he had visited
I heard him smile again
Much the same, much the same

he asked me where I was
Kildare, Ireland
what time it was
3.15am
he was amazed
said I should be asleep
I let that pass
asked me why I picked up the phone
at 3.15am

I told him that I picked it up
because it rang
he considered that
accepted it
apologised

I told him that it was okay
that it's not every day
or night
I get a call from a superhero
we hung it up then
3.20am
Flash never called again
nor any other superheroes
it was as good a call as any
and sleep
came easy
after

'Ladies and Gentlemen, We Interrupt This Programme...'

Orson Wells terrified the world in 1938
announcing the arrival
of Martians
or more accurately
the invasion
of Earth
by Martians

long before that there were cave wall paintings
worship for and offerings to
beings from outer space

more recently has been the declassification
of secret bases and millions of pages
of eyewitness accounts
abductions and encounters
all tinged with suspicion
sometimes horror

yet, there is no evidence
no concrete conclusion
no reason to suspect the existence
of life elsewhere and maybe
the real horror, the real terror

lies in the questions, not the answers

what if
there is nothing out there
what if
we are all alone
what if
there is only us

Flimflam

On the first day we just watched it
the three of us, amazed
at how it navigated its way
around the kitchen
under the table
around the chair legs
in clean figure-of-eights
a robot vacuum cleaner
the future really is now

on the second day we watched it again
how cleverly it went from the hall
to the bedrooms
patterning the nap of the carpet
criss-crosses and zigzags
its sensors slowing it down
turning it around
as it approached the skirting boards

on the third day my daughter gave it a name
Flimflam
or something

Flimflam came to help
does a good job

and in return
we empty the dust compartment
when it fills
clean the filters
when required
charge it
when it is done

our only job now
before unleashing Flimflam
is to remove items from the floor
clothes, shoes, the phone wires
a thirty second tidy

though some days
I can't be bothered
even to do that

They Can Do Great Things Now

They can do great things now
is what people say
I wonder if *they*
are working
on a tablet
that can burn/remove/delete
meaningless, pointless memories
tying our shoelaces
cleaning our teeth
walking
from here
to there
and back
again

I wonder if we still have it in us
to fill the spaces
that would
be left behind
I think we do
I hope we do

sometimes I don't want you
to look at me
and yet

it hurts
when you look away

I think we do

I hope we do

Driveway Masterpiece

Our fingertips are blue
pink, yellow and green
chalk dust

we have patterned the driveway
with stars and rainbows
hopscotch grids and huge words

messages for people
looking down from airplanes
aliens looking down from spaceships

she wonders what we might do next
I suggest making the tires on my car
colourful and pretty

we each take a tire
cover it with flowers and clouds and
for some reason, a cat

on the two rear tires
she suggests spirals
we get to work

we stand up, survey it all

happy even though
we know the rain will take it

she turns to me
a worried look on her face
I ask her why

she says that when we drive
the spirals will spin
that people will be hypnotised

I tell her not to worry
that most of them
already are

A.I.

The nonsense comes on at 2am
when I am just about to hit the sack
I always have a quick run-through
shopping channels flogging extendable hoses
electric bicycles and ab rollers
music channels with no music
documentaries on serial killers
competitive cooking programmes
and last night
a scientist
talking about the present
and the future
of artificial intelligence
it is a curious term
artificial intelligence
as if there is any other kind
as if our intelligence
the little we possess
was not created
is not artificial

yet we are creators now
edging closer
to creating our own sentient things
using intelligence received

from cosmic anomalies
received in turn
from someone, something
and so
we are gods

last week I read a story about a little girl
a toddler really
who had been tortured
from day one
in all of the ways
by her mother and her father
until her body gave out
and her parents stood before a judge
offering no reason
no remorse

we don't just cause the wounds
we prod them
spit in them
there is no doubt
no doubt at all
we are gods, we are gods

Comets and Moons and Whole Worlds

A long day
a long drive home
I carve through towns and villages
see old ladies carrying plastic bags
they lean into the wind and the rain
and the cold and the night
as they make their way
home
to put the dinner on
boil the kettle
to call a sister
on the phone
to compare days and months
and years and lives
unaware that they are galaxies
that comets and moons and whole worlds
came from them
move inside them still

I coast to a stop on the driveway
pull up the handbrake
watch raindrops trickle down the windscreen
taking with them
all of the stars

The Letter

Bills and junk mail
that's about the extent of it
usually

today, I received a letter
written
in a vaguely familiar hand

it was not threatening exactly
though it was unsettling
mentioning, as it did

things personal to me
thoughts
personal to me

my wife was named
our daughter too
I did not like it

I did not like
any of it
though I read it many times

it pleaded with me

to try to remember
how to be happy

to try to remember
how easy it can be
to let the world turn

as it has
before me
as it will after

it was postmarked
years
into the future

and
the signature
was my own

The Voice

The panic rises through him
swells of dark pressure
several times a day

he has fought against it often
but now
finds it to be
a kind of comfort

something to be welcomed
to give in to
a way of letting go

he is unsure of many things
the trivial now impossible
the faces surrounding him
having become
unfamiliar

there was a voice this morning
when he woke
the words were not important
only the resonance, the soft swaying rhythm

he listens to the voice

as he sits
in his armchair, and though
he finds it soothing
he is unsure
from where it emanates

part of him believing
that it comes
from within himself

part of him believing
that it comes
from a hidden corner of the universe

as if
there is a difference

Infinity

After midnight
still warm

there is no moon
no stars

nothing at all
to remind us

of infinity
or its opposite

Acknowledgements

A.I. *previously published by* Amsterdam Quarterly
An Understanding *previously published by* House of Zolo
Comets and Moons and Whole Worlds *previously published by* Fevers of the Mind
Curio *previously published by* Selcouth Station
Dizzy *previously published in* Secret Chords: A Poetry Anthology of the Best of the Folklore Prize
Galaxies *previously published in* The Poet Community Anthology
Howling at the Moon in 1957 *previously published by* Howl New Irish Writing
The Crevasse *previously published by* Strange Horizons
The Purple Flower *previously published by* Solarpunk Magazine
The Robot and Popcorn Ice Cream *previously published by* Dreich Magazine
The Voice *previously published by* York Literary Review
Time Machines and Laser Beams *previously published by* NewMyth

About the Author

Steve Denehan lives in Kildare, Ireland with his wife Eimear and daughter Robin. He is the author of two chapbooks and five poetry collections. Winner of the Anthony Cronin Poetry Award and twice winner of *Irish Times*' New Irish Writing, his numerous publication credits include *Poetry Ireland Review* and *Westerly*.

About the Publishing Team

Nate Ragolia is a lifelong lover of science fiction and its power to imagine worlds more hopeful and inclusive than the real one. His first book, *There You Feel Free*, was published by 1888's Black Hill Press in 2015. Spaceboy Books reissued it in 2021. He's also the author of *The Retroactivist* (2017). His most recent book, *One Person Can't Make a Difference* (2022), was featured on Tor.com's Can't Miss Indie Press Speculative Fiction list, and was translated into Italian for Ringworld Sci-Fi in 2023. He founded and edited *BONED*, a literary magazine, and also created two webcomics. Nate is also a husband and a dog dad.

Shaunn Grulkowski has been compared to Warren Ellis and Phillip K. Dick and was once described as what a baby conceived by Kurt Vonnegut and Margaret Atwood would turn out to be. He's at least the fifth best Slavic-Latino-American sci-fi writer in the Baltimore metro area. He's the author *Retcontinuum*, and the editor of *A Stalled Ox* and *The Goldfish* for 1888/Black Hill Press.